W9-AZS-511

USING THIS BOOK

*Children learn to read by **reading**, but they need help to begin.*

When you have read the story on the left-hand pages aloud to the child, go back to the beginning of the book and look at the pictures together.

Encourage children to read the sentences under the pictures. If they don't know a word, give them a chance to "guess" what it is from the illustrations before telling them.

There are more suggestions for helping children learn to read in the *Parent/Teacher Guide*.

A book for us
to read together,
little ladybug
Love,
Mommy and
Daddy

LADYBIRD BOOKS, INC.
Lewiston, Maine 04240 U.S.A.
© Text and layout SHEILA McCULLAGH MCMLXXXV
© In publication LADYBIRD BOOKS LTD MCMLXXXV
Loughborough, Leicestershire, England

All rights reserved. No part of this publication may be reproduced, stored in a retrieval system, or transmitted in any form or by any means, electronic, mechanical, photocopying, recording or otherwise, without the prior consent of the copyright owners.

Printed in England

October 6, 1988

The Dragon's Egg

written by SHEILA McCULLAGH
illustrated by JON DAVIS

This book belongs to:

Lara Kappler

Ladybird Books

The Magician lived in the old house
at the end of Puddle Lane.
One day, he saw a strange egg
in Mr. Wideawake's toy store.
He bought the egg, and
took it home.

The Magician
took the egg home.

He put it on a shelf in his room.

The sun shone in through the window.

It shone on the strange egg.

The egg grew warm in the sunshine.

One day, a little crack appeared
in the side of the egg.

The Magician didn't notice the crack.

He was very busy,
writing a book about magic,
and he forgot to look.

There was a crack
in the egg.
The Magician didn't
notice the crack.

The very next day,
when the Magician was out,
the crack in the egg grew wider.
A little bit of eggshell fell in.
A puff of smoke came
out of the hole.
It was followed by a long, scaly head,
and a little dragon looked out.

A little dragon
looked out of the hole.

Slowly, the little dragon
pulled himself out of the egg.
He opened his jaws, and yawned.
A flash of fire came out of his mouth,
followed by a puff of smoke.

The little dragon
pulled himself
out of the egg.

The sun shone on the dragon's wings.
He opened his wings wide
in the sunshine.
The window was open.
The dragon flew to the open window.

The dragon flew
to the open window.

The little dragon looked down
into the garden.
He saw two little mice,
sitting on an overturned flowerpot.

The little dragon looked down
into the garden.

He saw two little mice.

The dragon was hungry.
He spread his wings, and
flew down into the garden.
He flew straight toward
the two little mice.
But at that moment, the mice looked up
and saw the dragon coming.
Quick as a flash,
they tumbled through the hole
into the flowerpot.
They were just in time.

The dragon was hungry.

He flew down into the garden.

The dragon landed
on top of the flowerpot.
(He was a very little dragon.)
The two little mice were hiding inside.
They looked up.
They saw the dragon's eye
looking at them.
They were very frightened.

The two little mice looked up.

They saw the dragon's eye
looking at them.

The little dragon took a deep breath.
He was just about to puff
fire and smoke into the flowerpot,
when he felt himself being lifted
into the air.
He turned his head, and
saw the Magician.

The little dragon
saw the Magician.

"So that's what the egg was!"
said the Magician.
"A dragon's egg!
I might have known!"

"Let me go!" cried the little dragon.
Fire and smoke poured out of his jaws,
but the Magician held him tight.
"You must learn to behave,"
said the Magician.
"You can't go around
frightening people like this!"

"But I'm hungry!" hissed the dragon.

"Are you, now?" said the Magician.
"Well, you won't eat the creatures
who live in **my** garden!"

"Let me go!"
cried the little dragon.

The Magician took the dragon
into the house.
He went upstairs to the attic.
He put the little dragon
into an iron cage,
and gave him an egg for breakfast.

As soon as they were sure
that the dragon was gone,
the two little mice ran home
to a hole under the tree.

The Magician took
the dragon
into the house.

He put the little dragon
into a cage.

The Magician looked out the window.
He saw the Griffle in the garden,
and called to him.
(The Griffle was a friendly monster.)
"Go and see the mice,"
he said to the Griffle.
"Go and see the cats,
who live under the steps,
and the owl who lives
in one of the attic rooms.
Tell them all to come here
at seven o'clock this evening."

The Magician
said to the Griffle,
"Go and see the mice,
the cats, and the owl.
Tell them to come here
at seven o'clock."

The Griffle went into the attic room,
where the barn owl was fast asleep.
"Wake up, owl," said the Griffle.
"You must go and see the Magician
at seven o'clock."
The big barn owl
opened one eye.
"Too-whit, too-whoo-oo!"
he said.

He shut his eye, and
went back to sleep.

"Wake up, owl,"
said the Griffle.
"You must go and
see the Magician
at seven o'clock."

The Griffle went out into the garden.
He looked into the hole
under the steps, and he saw
three little cats, all fast asleep.
"Wake up, cats," said the Griffle.
"You must go and see the Magician
at seven o'clock."
The three little cats all opened their eyes
and sat up.
"We'll be there," they all said together.

"Wake up, cats,"
said the Griffle.
"You must go and
see the Magician
at seven o'clock."

The mice all lived in a big hole
under the hollow tree.
The Griffle was afraid of mice,
so he didn't go to see them.
He wrote a note
on a piece of paper,
and dropped it into the tree.
The note said,
"You must all go and
see the Magician
at seven o'clock."

The note said,
"You must all go and
see the Magician
at seven o'clock."

Grandfather Mouse found the note.
Fortunately, Grandfather Mouse
had learned to read from the labels
in Mr. Wideawake's toy store.
So he read the note aloud
to the other mice.
"We must all go,"
said Grandfather Mouse.

"But we don't know the way,"
said Uncle Maximus.

"I do," said Chestnut Mouse.
"I'll show you."

You must all go and see the Magician at seven o'clock

"We must all go,"
said Grandfather Mouse.

At seven o'clock, the Magician
was sitting in his chair in his room.
As the clock struck seven,
three little cats climbed
down a pole from the open skylight.
Eight little mice came up
from a hole in the floorboard.
The barn owl flew in
through the window.
"Good," said the Magician.
"You are all here."

The Magician said,
"Good. You are all here."

"You must all listen very carefully,"
said the Magician.
"If you want to go on
living in my garden,
you must all make a promise.
You must promise not to eat
anyone else who lives in the garden."

"We promise," cried the little mice,
before anyone else had time to speak.

The Magician said,
''You must all promise
not to eat anyone
in the garden.''

"Can we eat the mice
when they're **not** in the garden?"
asked one of the cats.
The mice all shivered, and
looked at one another.
"I'd rather you didn't,"
said the Magician.

"All right," said the cats. "We won't.
We promise."

"Owl?" asked the Magician.

"I promise, too.
Too-whit, too-whoo!"
said the owl.

"We promise," said the cats.
"I promise, too," said the owl.

"I'll promise, too, if you let me go,"
said the dragon.

"No," said the Magician.
"I never trust promises made by dragons.
You will stay where you are,
till I have had time to make magic.
I must make some strong magic
against dragons."

The dragon said,
''I will promise, too,
if you let me go.''
''No,'' said the Magician.

Notes for the parent/teacher

Turn back to the beginning, and print the child's name in the space on the title page, using ordinary, not capital letters.

Now go through the book again. Look at each picture and talk about it. Point to the caption below, and read it aloud yourself.

Run your finger under the words as you read, so that the child learns that reading goes from left to right.

Encourage the child to read the words under the illustrations. Don't rush in with the word before he/she has had time to think, but don't leave him/her struggling.

Read this story as often as the child likes hearing it. The more opportunities he/she has to look at the illustrations and **read** the captions with you, the more he/she will come to recognize the words.

If you have several books, let the child choose which story he/she would like.

Grandfather Mouse stirred.
He shook the magic dust from his head,
and took a step forward.
"I can move!" he cried.
"I can talk, too!"
"So can I!" said Grandmother Mouse.
(She sounded very surprised.)

Grandfather Mouse
and
Grandmother Mouse